LIKE A
TROPHY
FROM
THE SUN

ESSENTIAL POETS SERIES 311

Guernica Editions Inc. acknowledges the support of
the Canada Council for the Arts and the Ontario Arts Council.
The Ontario Arts Council is an agency of the Government of Ontario.

We acknowledge the financial support of the Government of Canada.

Jason
Heroux

LIKE A
TROPHY
FROM
THE SUN

GUERNICA
EDITIONS
TORONTO • CHICAGO
BUFFALO • LANCASTER (U.K.)
2024

Guernica Founder: Antonio D'Alfonso

Michael Mirolla, editor
Cover and interior design: Rafael Chimicatti
Cover image: fran_kie/Shutterstock.com

Guernica Editions Inc.
1241 Marble Rock Rd., Gananoque, (ON), Canada K7G 2V4
2250 Military Road, Tonawanda, N.Y. 14150-6000 U.S.A.
www.guernicaeditions.com

Distributors:
University of Toronto Press Distribution (UTP)
5201 Dufferin Street, Toronto (ON), Canada M3H 5T8
Independent Publishers Group (IPG)
814 N Franklin Street, Chicago, IL 60610, U.S.A.

First edition.
Printed in Canada.

Legal Deposit – Third Quarter
Library of Congress Catalogue Card Number: 2024931055
Library and Archives Canada Cataloguing in Publication
Title: Like a trophy from the sun / Jason Heroux.
Names: Heroux, Jason, author.
Series: Essential poets ; 311.
Description: Series statement: Essential poets series ; 311
Identifiers: Canadiana 2024028965X | ISBN 9781771839020 (softcover)
Subjects: LCGFT: Poetry.
Classification: LCC PS8565.E825 L55 2024 | DDC C811/.6—dc23

Denne boka er til Dag T. Straumsvåg

CONTENTS

*Our life is no dream,
but it should and will perhaps become one.*
—NOVALIS

I travelled to a half-finished place. None of the fruits were ripe enough to eat. Houses had doorways but no doors. The people there asked what one plus one equalled. They were a very sad people. No joke ever reached its punch line. The air was full of insects that never died.

Life soldiers on, and on the bus I overheard some-
one say, *even dead leaves look and sound leaf-like
if there's enough wind.* Birds are buckets of song
raised from a well. The moon is a bucket of light.
Pet speck of dust, where's your leash? Let's go for
a walk.

This evening at the bus-stop pale steam rose from my coffee cup, spreading its wings like a blind white bat from the mouth of a Styrofoam cave. Not everything that breaks needs to be repaired or replaced. Lend us a puddle for our rain. Let us borrow another tomorrow, another parade. Another gently lost paddle for the bottom of our lake. The moon is leaving town, having a yard sale in the sky, selling its gently used light. The orange-people are peeled by the hand-people. A rain-person disappears into the gutter-person. At the end of the day a bicycle-beast is chained to the streetlamp. Good morning butchers, washing your hands in our hearts. Goodnight dark empty shoe hopping through the woods.

This is your captain weeping, the pilot announced, sobbing from the cockpit as we flew through a storm. Eddies of air rattled the cabin. Emergency lights flickered. *Even the most experienced jam maker has an off day now and then*, a voice whispered behind the First Class curtain. A two-headed stewardess walked along the center aisle. One head assured us everything was fine, but the other head admitted we were all going to die. Both heads were right but one was wrong.

The tour guide showed our group the local sights. He pointed to himself. *I am the tour guide.* He pointed overhead. *That is the sky.* He pointed to the past. *That was long ago.* The tour went on and on. Eventually I was the only one left in the group. He pointed to an unfamiliar house across the street. *Hey, there's where you live.* I followed him inside. He pointed to two people I'd never seen before. *This must be your wife and child.* My child smiled. He showed me his sore tooth. According to the brochure this was the happiest I'd ever been. My wife played our song and danced with the guide. I took it all in.

In the only world I ever lived in I learned a horse's skeleton has one less bone than a human skeleton and an ounce of pain on earth weighs the same as an ounce of earth. I saw someone's chimney smoke rise like the grey spirit of a dead shoelace. Some of what I did I wanted to do. Some of what I said I meant. My own beaten heart knew happiness like the back of its hand. But what I truly miss most is seeing the crowded city buses drifting like clouds carrying human rain, human snow.

Bless the one who carries a bag of fresh raindrops feeding the puddles. Bless the onionskin lying awake in the garbage bag without its onion. Bless the prescription for rain written by a cloud to help the horse calm down. Bless the elderly shoelace threaded through the open eyelets of newborn shoes. Bless the shivering star shining like a silver sardine dreaming in its tin. Bless the stones without customer service skills that end up fired from the world. Bless the breadcrumbs afraid of brooms that still march in the breadcrumb parade. Bless the specks of dust on windowsills discussing the past still to come. Bless the broken sunset unravelling like a golden cassette in the horizon's tape deck. Bless the short grey living scarf of the squirrel warming the power line's neck. Bless the soft kitten paws of summer traffic playing with the road's black string.

I flew a paper plane. It glided through the paper sky until it crashed into the paper sea. Someone called my name and said it was nearly time for dinner, but I was alone. I stood on my front porch, lost. When I hear the voice of someone who isn't there, which one of us is the ghost? The silence of the stars, like their light, can take years to reach our ears.

Early spring morning give yourself a chance. Whatever is coming can wait. You're stronger than you think. Stand your ground, stay a while so we can catch up like old friends. What's new with you these days? Tell me again how your silk nests are spun in cherry trees along the highway. Show me the gentle sleepy wind curled-up like a newborn kitten in your hand.

Hello today, how is everything going? I woke up within you. I heard your baby sunlight say its first golden gaga goo-goo. Like a great explorer from the past I discovered the rivers of my arms flowed into the lakes of my hands. The tree in the backyard played with its friends, a street with no arms or legs slithered home. Goodbye, I am an eight-legged light bulb repairing my broken lamp in the sky.

After many years I dreamt I came back to life as the newly renovated central branch of the Kingston Frontenac Public Library downtown on Johnson between Bagot and Wellington. It was late at night. By the time I arrived I was closed. I didn't know what to do. I didn't know where to go, so I woke up and walked back home. *I've never seen anything like it*, a blind street corner astrologer said under a dark and starry sky.

It began with a tuxedo hanging next to an evening gown. They fell in love, started a family. Baby clothes appeared. The population grew. Pajamas. Overalls. Swimwear. Police uniforms. Hospital robes. A town of outfits went about their business in the closet, day after day. No one ironed them. No one wore them. No one packed them in a suitcase for a surprise vacation. The only heartbeat among them belonged to a moth, fluttering back and forth. *I think tomorrow is my funeral*, a left shoe whispered. *Mine too*, the right one agreed.

Dear R, it's evening here in Kingston at the moment. Is it evening in Orillia? If it is, it's a different evening. Not the same one that I'm writing about, because the one I'm writing about is already gone, a thing of the past. Your evening is in the future. What are things like in the future? Has anyone built a raindrop that drops by itself, with no cloud required? Has anyone invented a new way to peel a banana? Here in the past not much has changed. The expired milk remains expired. The rust grows rustier. Take care.

My grandfather owned a pillow farm. He made a fortune ripping them apart and selling their feathers. But no one wants to hear about that. No one wants to hear how during those dark days when you slept there was no place to lay your head. Ghosts wandered the halls like blank pages torn from a book. Sometimes late at night we heard them crying to be turned.

I mostly enjoyed life, even when pushing a shopping cart through the aisles. The shelves were often bare. Other people's carts were usually full. I saw what I needed in theirs. They saw what they wanted in mine. A woman passed by, removed a can of salmon from my cart, and added it to hers. When I tried to take it back I grabbed a jar of jam by mistake. I didn't need jam. Didn't care for it. I placed the jam in an old man's cart, and grabbed his bag of apples. But he snatched his apples back, returned my jam. Then he took my milk. My butter. My eggs. I waited in line with an empty cart and at the end of the day when it came time to pay I still couldn't afford what it cost.

I woke up in my pocket. Ate lint to survive. Keys grew on trees, obviously, but locks were very rare. It snowed light, rained sand. Hours turned into years. Years became days. I read old receipts like scripture. Sometimes a hand from head office arrived to make deliveries, shuffled items around, took smoke breaks. Mostly I was alone. The moon glowed in the sky like a shiny quarter set aside for bus fare.

One day the Master and the student wandered through the woods. After eight hours the Master asked, *Where are we?* The student said nothing. The Master said, *Wrong.* The next day the Master and the student wandered through the woods. After eight hours the Master asked, *Where are we?* The student said nothing. The Master said, *Bingo.*

The body is the envelope and the spirit is the letter within, or the spirit is the envelope and the body is within, the Office Depot sales clerk told me in the stationery aisle. *Either way, the letter gives the envelope purpose. Without the letter the envelope has nothing to envelop.* I asked the clerk what happens next, but he didn't know. He called his manager over to explain. *When the letter slips into the envelope and the envelope is sealed, they are one*, the manager said. *And as one they move through the world. And reach another.* The manager wasn't sure how things worked from there. He advised me to call Head Office. *For the letter to fully be received the envelope must be opened, the seal broken*, a voice from Head Office whispered to me over the phone. *And that's pretty much how the journey always ends, open, broken, in someone's hands.*

Ghosts do nothing on their own. They are like memories that have forgotten where they belong. You remembered that when you came home and saw your brother. He asked who you were. You said you were your brother. The two of you sat on the damaged porch, a cool wind looked for a place to hide. *If you're your brother, then who am I?* your brother asked. You told him he was his own brother. There was no cloud in the sky, no sky. *If I'm my brother, then how come I'm not home?* your brother asked. A local factory smoked. You tasted the air in the air, as if it was bad. He asked you again why he wasn't home. You said it was because he moved. A piece of dirt lay dying in the grass. It felt alone. *But why did I move?* he asked. *Where did I go?*

Did I ever tell you about the time the telephone rang with a wrong number? An old woman trying to reach the Ambassador Hotel requested I connect her to room 412. No one had ever asked me to do that before. I didn't know how to connect a call. I wasn't even sure where the Ambassador Hotel was. The old woman sensed my confusion. She asked if I was new, and I said I was. She wondered if there was anyone else around to help. I said no, there wasn't. I was the only one here. *I'll call back later when you're not so alone*, she said, and hung up. I never heard from her again.

Hey body, remember when you made me clean and dress myself and listen to the birds singing in the old linden tree? I didn't want to hear birds. You made me listen. You made me tired. You made me dream. You woke me up. You needed me to keep you company until you wanted to be alone and when you asked me to go away I went.

It was the greatest show on earth but no one witnessed it. I sat alone in the audience, watching an empty stage. After a few hours I realized it was 1767. Circuses weren't invented yet. But somehow I still knew the show had to go on. I walked into the centre ring and sawed myself in half. My spilled organs steamed upon the straw-covered floor. Then one half of me clowned around with the other. One half of me juggled the other. I gathered my strength. I took a bow.

Many things were possessed by devils in olden days, but devils have less time now, so everything must possess itself. Puddles possessed by raindrops. The colour green possessed by the ghosts of yellow and blue, the early morning sky possessed by the hope of things to come. Last night I possessed my room to go dark after I switched off the light. *The whole world is haunted*, my dead grandmother said, carrying a tray of stale biscuits through the woods. The wind hurried past, like a dog playing fetch with my breath. I lost track of time. A minute went by, and then three years, and then another minute. *Pencil sharpeners were banned during the war for wasting valuable wood shavings*, a possessed pencil stub whispered behind my ear.

In a previous life I was a Norman Rockwell calendar. I don't remember January. In February I was a single glass of orange soda with two straws, sipped by young sweethearts. I don't remember March. In April I was a child with my face pressed up against a pane of glass gazing upon the bald-headed master watchmaker. I don't remember May. I don't remember June. In July I was on the moon. My heart weighed the same as a golf ball. When August rolled around I was a woman sitting at the kitchen table as the sun went down. Repairing old electric lamps with my eyes closed. I don't remember September. I don't remember October. I don't remember November. I don't remember December.

When I went to the hospital to visit my friend I saw the hospital was torn down, demolished, replaced by an auto repair garage. The reception-ist led me into the main bay. Someone dressed in a mechanic's jumpsuit stood near the hydraulic lift, wiping his hands with a greasy rag. *He wants to see his friend*, the receptionist said. *He can't*, the mechanic replied. The receptionist looked at me, shook her head. *You can't*. I asked why not. The receptionist glanced at the mechanic. *Why can't he?* The mechanic continued wiping his hands. *Because it's not possible.*

I found an old joy journal containing handwritten entries of enjoyable moments, like crossing an empty intersection alone in the early morning. Seeing ducks on the water, ducks in the grass. Taking the garbage out to the edge of the yard under the stars. Hearing the other side of your voice laughing for no reason. The evening light against a wall, a stranger's kind wave, the softness of Pablo's fur. Breathing the air one day. Breathing the air another day.

There was a knock at the door. I opened it. I saw a person. I still heard the knocking. It came from inside the person. I opened the person. There was a heart. I pressed my ear against it and heard knocking within. I opened the heart. I saw a door. Another door. And another. It was like a village of tiny doors living inside the heart. *Please don't tell anyone we're here*, one of the doors said. *We have nowhere else to go.*

We carried chairs with us everywhere we went. Distant music played in the air. Birds sang in the trees. The river babbled in its bed. If the music stopped we had to sit. I was lucky, my chair was a lightweight plastic patio piece, easy to move. My father carried a heavy wooden rocking chair. He struggled with every step. The last time I saw him he'd been dead two years, but still looked the same. The music never stopped.

Our ghost town was like all the others. Empty birdcages broke into song every morning. A basketball bounced back and forth across the court by itself. The weatherman on his deathbed whispered it looked like rain, but the sky was clear. Sometimes late at night it got so quiet you could hear your own ears. I found my ghost hiding in the shed, naked, and shivering. He hadn't eaten for days. I explained everything was fine but he didn't believe me. The next day he was gone. I disappeared soon after. What sort of world is this? Nothing is safe, and yet somehow even now I still feel everything will be okay.

ACKNOWLEDGEMENTS

101 Words, Apocalypse Confidential, Arc, Blue-pepper, Carte Blanche, Gone Lawn, Juniper, Molecule, MoonPark Review, Revolution John, Sonic Boom, Sunrise with Sea Monsters, Talking About Strawberries All the Time, The Feathertale Review, The New Quarterly, Train Poetry Journal, Unbroken, ZIN Daily, *Goodnight Dark Empty Shoe Hopping Through the Woods, Marks of Cain, Notes from the All You Can Eat Buffet,* and *The Book of Blessings.*

ABOUT THE AUTHOR

Jason Heroux is the author of four books of poetry: *Memoirs of an Alias* (2004); *Emergency Hallelujah* (2008); *Natural Capital* (2012) and *Hard Work Cheering Up Sad Machines* (2016). His most recent book is the short story collection *Survivors of the Hive* (Radiant Press, 2023). Translated into French, Italian and Arabic, his poetry has been featured in several anthologies, including *Breathing Fire 2: Canada's New Poets*, and *Best Canadian Poetry in English 2008, 2011* and *2016*, and has appeared in magazines and journals in Canada, the U.S, Belgium, France, and Italy. He was the Poet Laureate for the City of Kingston, Ontario, from 2019 to 2022.

Printed by Imprimerie Gauvin
Gatineau, Québec